Raewyn Caisley

Illustrated by Anne Spudvilas

Contents

Chapter One
    Downhill Run *1*

Chapter Two
    Boom *6*

Chapter Three
    Memory-1-send *11*

Chapter Four
    Contact *19*

Chapter Five
    Fallout *26*

Chapter Six
    Cold and Alone *30*

Chapter Seven
    Rescue *35*

Chapter Eight
    Boy Phones for Help *39*

CHAPTER ONE
Downhill Run

I was making sure that my skis were still secure, stomping them in the snow like Dad taught me, when Micha whizzed past.

"Come on, Ben!" she called. "I'll race you to that rock. Last one to the marker gets a snowball!"

I dug my poles in again and tried to catch up. I wasn't as fast as Micha because I'd missed a couple of seasons.

My family hadn't been able to go skiing since Dad left his job to start up his own business. This trip sure made up for it, though! I mean, who would have thought I'd ever get to go skiing in New Zealand! I guess that's just what happens when your best friend has really generous parents.

We had been skiing with the grown-ups for a while, which wasn't much fun, when Micha told her dad, Mr. Lee, that we were going to ski to the bottom for a rest. Mr. Lee sent Martin, Micha's 18-year-old New Zealand cousin, with us. Micha and I grinned. At least it would be more like we were skiing by ourselves.

Everyone agreed to meet at the cafe at the end of the run at a quarter to four. Then Mr. Lee said, "You look after these two, 007."

Mr. Lee had started calling Martin "007" after he'd caught him clipping his mobile phone to his ski pants. Martin hadn't wanted to leave his brand new phone in the ski lodge.

"See you at the bottom!" Martin's mom had said. Then she and Mr. and Mrs. Lee had skied off around a bend.

So now it was just us. As I skied down with Micha, I thought about what Todd, my pain of a big brother, had said. He had been so jealous when he'd heard I was going skiing with the Lees that he'd told me all the ski slopes in New Zealand were on the sides of active volcanoes! It was great to escape his teasing for a while.

Of course, Martin wasn't letting me off, either. He was nearly as bad as Todd! When I'd asked him about what Todd had said, Martin had nodded seriously and said, "One minute you can be skiing along, and the next thing you know, you're stuck in hot lava and your legs are on fire!"

Luckily, what Martin had said was so stupid I'd known right away he was kidding. Then, when Martin's mom's new four-wheel-drive had rounded that corner and I'd caught my first glimpse of the beautiful snow-covered mountain, all my fears about volcanoes had vanished anyway. There it was, glistening coldly in the bright winter sun—a perfect picture postcard—except for its broken-off top.

If Mount Ruapehu (*Roo-ah-pay-hoo* as the New Zealanders say it) was a volcano, I'd decided, it certainly wasn't a hot one.

Chapter Two
Boom

Micha was waiting for me at the first marker.

"I beat you!" she said as I skidded to a stop.

"I'll beat you to the next one!" I called.

"I'll give you a head start, then!" she yelled.

Martin skied past us, keeping his distance. He said he was there to ski, not to play tag.

BOOM

I straightened my skis and took off. Then, just as I hit a small bump, it felt as if the earth shuddered.

"Hey, did you feel that?" I called to Micha as she flashed by.

"What?" Micha called back.

"Don't worry about it," I shouted.

She was going way too fast to have a conversation. Anyway, it was probably just my imagination. Micha was waiting for me again at the next marker.

"All right," I shouted. "I give up." I laughed, knowing I had just been beaten—but that was okay. Micha was my best friend and if it wasn't for her I wouldn't have been here skiing on the slopes of Mount Ruapehu anyway. I was happy to have her win.

Just then, Martin slid to an abrupt stop a couple of yards away, spraying snow in an arc.

"There's a really good ridge of snow over that hill," he said. "I'm going to try it. I'll just be a minute. You two wait here."

Martin skied over the crest of the hill. He was going as fast as he could across a small clearing.

Martin squatted on his skis and was getting ready to jump when Micha and I heard the boom. It sounded like a cruise missile had slammed into the side of Mount Ruapehu.

We looked up at the peak. As we watched, a huge, gray mushroom cloud billowed up out of the crater.

The cloud bubbled and grew like milk when it boils over. Then suddenly, a jet of pure black smoke shot straight up through the mushroom.

Another bang followed a split second later. We both jumped out of our skin. I couldn't take my eyes off the top of the mountain.

Then, over the terrible sound of the eruption, we heard Martin yell.

Chapter Three
Memory-1-send

We found Martin lying unconscious in the snow at the bottom of a small cliff, with his leg sticking out at a crazy angle and blood coming from a cut on his head.

Micha had screamed when she'd seen him like that, and she'd just stood there staring, afraid to go near him at first.

I'd gone over and knelt down beside Martin, only to realize I didn't have a clue what to do. Then Martin moaned and moved his hip slightly. That was when I saw the mobile phone.

I tried 911 first. A voice said that the number I had called wasn't connected.

I realized that the emergency number probably wasn't the same in New Zealand. Now what? Who should I call?

Suddenly Micha was beside me. "Try the numbers Martin's got programmed into the phone," she said. "I saw him saving his friends' numbers back at the lodge."

I tried the first number by pressing MEMORY-1-SEND.

"Please, let someone be home," I thought, listening to the ring.

"You've reached Greg and Sam's place," said a cheerful voice on the other end. "Leave us a message after the beep and we'll get back to you."

I looked at Micha. "It's an answering machine."

Micha rolled her eyes. "Hang up and try the next one."

I pressed the button that said END and tried again. MEMORY-2-SEND. This time, a girl's voice came on after a couple of rings.

"Jane Porter speaking."

"Hello!" Suddenly I didn't really know what else to say. "Look, you don't know me, but we're in trouble. We need your help. We're on the side of a volcano and it's erupting and Martin's had an accident. We don't know what to do."

I knew I was talking too fast and not making much sense.

"Is this some kind of joke?" the girl asked. "Well, it isn't very funny."

"No! It's not a joke," I shouted. "I mean it. We're on the side of Mount Ruapehu. We were skiing with Martin and there was this explosion and ..."

"Did you say you were with Martin?" the girl asked through the growing static on the line.

"Yes! That's right!" I yelled. "I'm Ben Cameron. I was skiing with Martin. He's hurt. There's something wrong with his leg. I think he must have hit his head." I looked up at the mountain.

The line went dead just as another huge cloud of smoke and ash blew into the sky.

Martin moaned and twitched his terribly crooked leg. I tried the same phone number again.

This time, as soon as the girl picked up the phone, I said, "LISTEN!"

There was another huge explosion, and a little way off a large, black rock landed, hissed, and sank into the snow.

"I think Martin's leg is broken. We were skiing. He went off by himself. He went over the edge into this gully. And it's true, the volcano is erupting!"

I was saying everything too quickly and shouting again.

"Hang on a minute," the girl said. "I'll go and get my first-aid book."

I could actually hear her run down the hall. Then she was back.

"Okay, I did first aid at summer camp. You have to make a splint for Martin's leg. Use your skis or some branches. Tie them around his leg so he can't move it. You need to put pressure on the bleeding as well, and, oh yeah, keep him warm! He'll be in shock."

Then, just as I was about to ask her to repeat what she'd said, the phone went dead again.

Chapter Four
Contact

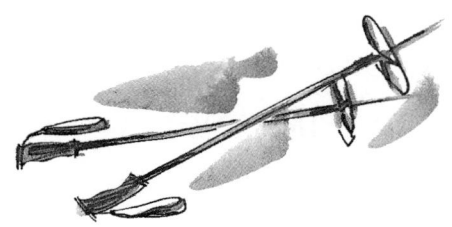

I looked around. There weren't any trees, not up that high, and Martin's skis were too long. So much for the splint.

"We have to keep him warm," I told Micha. "And we're supposed to do something to stop the bleeding."

"Okay," said Micha in a wobbly voice. She took off her headband.

"We could use this for his head. It's just like a bandage."

"Great," I said. "But how do we get it on him?"

"You hold the front," said Micha, and she gently wriggled the elastic headband over Martin's head. Next, she pulled a travel pack of tissues out of her pocket and tucked the whole wad under the headband. It wasn't pretty, but it looked like it would work.

"Hey, that's great," I said with real admiration. A minute before, Micha had been too afraid to touch her cousin, and now she was like a regular doctor!

I took off my ski jacket and laid it on Martin, not looking at his crooked leg. Then the phone rang.

"Hello!" I said, but the phone kept on ringing. I realized I didn't know how to answer it. Micha leaned over and pressed a button. I put the phone to my ear.

"Ben Cameron?" came a man's voice with a New Zealand accent.

I just said, "Yes."

"It's Jim Saunders, Ben. I'm with the park rangers. We've just had a call from a girl named Jane Porter in Auckland, and we've got your friend Micha's family here with us. Are you all right? Can you tell me what's happened?"

Another explosion made me look up, and to my horror, I saw the crater overflowing with something black. A stream of the black stuff was heading down in our direction. I spoke into the phone, explaining everything again.

"And now there's lava coming straight for us!"

"Okay, Ben. Slow down, son," said Jim. "Take a deep breath."

I took a deep, shuddering breath. I looked over at Micha. She'd taken off her ski jacket and laid it over Martin, too. His lips were turning blue.

"It's not lava. It's a mud flow, and that's good because it will help us to figure out where you are," said Jim. "We're sending a team up right now. I want you to guide them. First, I want you to tell me a little bit about Martin. Is he awake?"

I said Martin's name. His eyes were still closed. "I think he's sleeping," I said. Then it struck me that lying in snow was a funny place to sleep.

"Give him a shake," said Jim.

"But I might hurt him."

"Just give him a nudge and call out his name."

I took hold of Martin's shoulder and gave him a gentle shake.

"Hey! What do you think you're doing?" asked Micha.

"I have to do it," I said. "That's what the guy told me."

"Martin," I said, quietly. Then, I said it again, louder.

"He won't wake up!" I yelled into the phone. "Is he . . .?"

Micha let out a horrified yelp.

"Put your face up to his mouth and see if he's breathing," said Jim.

I leaned over. I could feel Martin's warm breath tickling my cheek.

"HE'S BREATHING!" I yelled.

Chapter Five
Fallout

"That's good, Ben," said the park ranger. "Now, what you have to do is keep him warm."

I was starting to shiver myself. I only had a sweater and ski pants on.

"We've given him our ski jackets," I said into the phone.

"There's no point in you two freezing as well, son," said Jim. "Curl up next to him under your ski jackets and snuggle up to him as close as you can. Body heat's the best thing. Rub his arms, too, to keep the blood flowing."

I told Micha what the park ranger said. I put the phone down in the snow and we both rubbed Martin's arms. They felt cold and rubbery. His eyelids fluttered as we curled up beside him.

I picked up the phone again with my free hand, but just as I did, I heard a loud bang, and half a dozen big stones landed in the snow. It was like the mountain was throwing fistfuls of gravel at us.

"Hello," I said, but I could only hear static. Then, way off in the distance, I heard the park ranger.

"Okay, now, Ben, I need you to tell me, as clearly as you can, exactly where you are . . ."

"Hello!" I said again. "Can you hear me? HELLO! HELLO!"

The park ranger was gone. All I could hear was fizzing and crackling. I put the phone down and snuggled up as close as I could possibly get to Micha and Martin.

Lying with my head against the side of the mountain was like listening to somebody's stomach growl. Mount Ruapehu rumbled and gurgled beneath us.

Chapter Six
Cold and Alone

It seemed like we lay on the side of the volcano for a very long time.

The phone rang twice. Once there was only static, but the second time, when Micha answered, she said she heard bits of words and sentences before the line went dead. Micha said it sounded like Martin's mom, but she couldn't understand anything.

The two of us snuggled as close to Martin as we could. I reached across the top of Martin and took hold of Micha's hand to try and comfort her. It was frightening when Martin moaned, and I could only imagine that Micha was twice as scared as I was. Martin didn't seem to be getting any warmer, either. His face was deathly pale.

My left arm was in the snow, and it ached with the cold. The sleeve of my sweater was soaked through and the wetness was spreading down my side and across my back.

In the meantime, the volcano kept on erupting, and every so often we were pelted with hot stones.

Once, a stone the size of a quarter landed on my ski jacket. It melted through the material in a second and I had to throw the jacket off. When I

COLD AND ALONE

curled up underneath it again, it was all wet. I shivered uncontrollably.

Then, just as I felt a lump welling up in my throat that I couldn't quite swallow, I looked down the mountain and saw three people coming toward us.

They were towing bright orange stretchers. Two were dressed in overalls of the same bright color. The other wore a blue, woolen ski hat with stars and stripes on it.

I choked on a little cry of relief and got to my feet. I waved the mobile phone wildly with my good arm. My left arm felt like a dead, frozen fish by my side.

"Micha!" I said. "Micha. It's your dad!"

Chapter Seven
Rescue

Wrapped in thick woolen blankets, we watched as Mr. Lee and the rangers took care of Martin.

First they slipped his leg into a long, plastic sock that blew up like a beach ball. Then they gently lifted him onto one of the stretchers and covered him with some shiny silver material.

"Your turn, guys," said Mr. Lee. He was pointing to the other two bright orange stretchers.

"I'm all right, Mr. Lee. I can ski down," I said.

"Yeah, so can I, Dad," said Micha.

Mr. Lee gathered up our poles and skis as one of the rangers slid into the harness on Martin's stretcher.

"I bet you guys could do anything you set your minds to," said Mr. Lee. "But this will be quicker."

He wrapped more of the silver material around us. The ground gave a violent shudder.

"I think we'd better beat it."

Mr. Lee held one stretcher still as I climbed in and lay down. The other ranger held a stretcher for Micha. We both grinned at each other, lying there like two smiling, silver caterpillars.

"Better not forget this," said Mr. Lee, and he tucked the mobile phone into the pocket of my ski jacket.

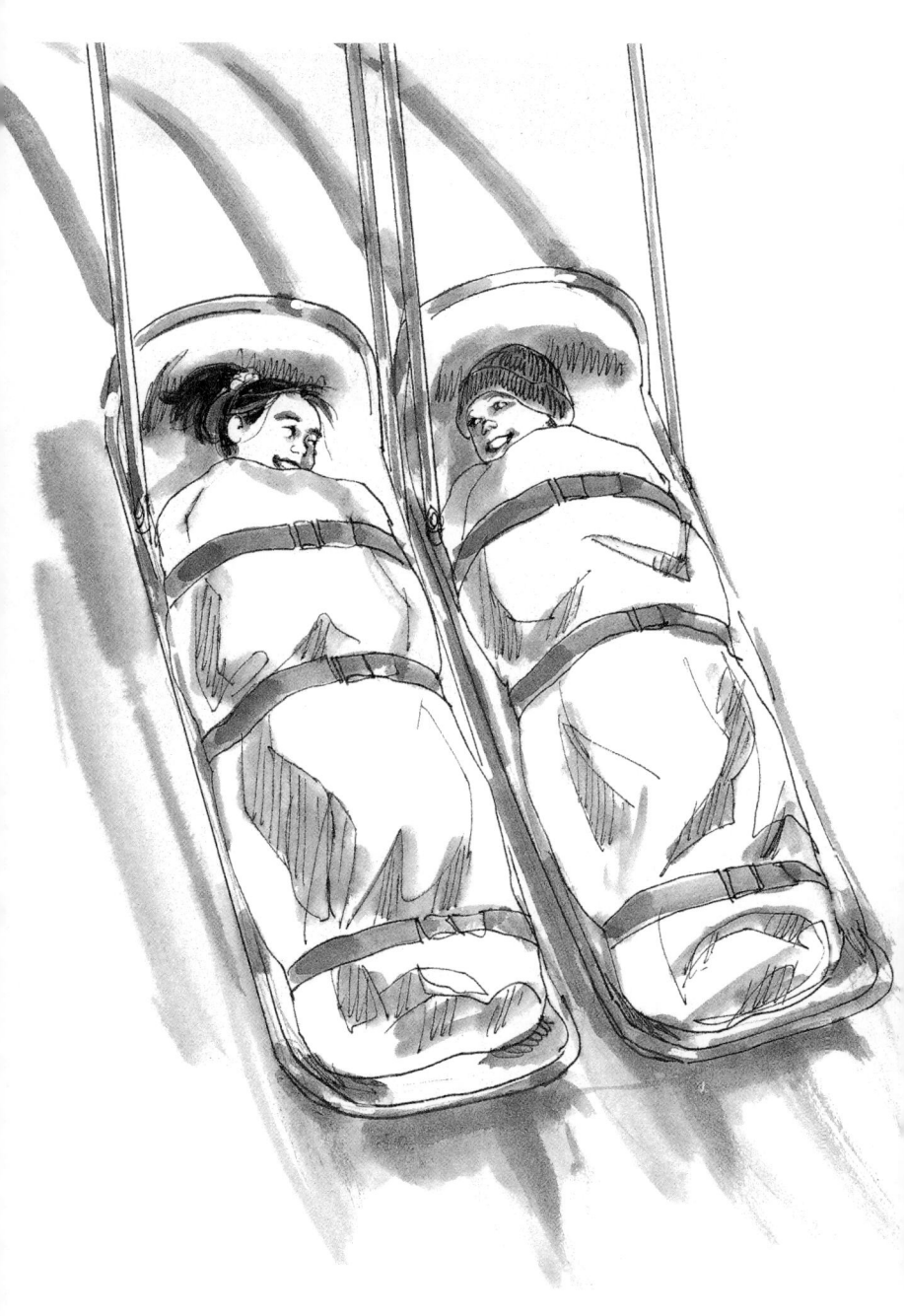

As we slid through the snow in our cozy cocoons, I looked back up at the mountain.

It was black all around the rim of the crater—nothing like the clean white peak it had been earlier—and the sun couldn't shine through the thick cloud of smoke.

How wrong could a guy be . . .

CHAPTER EIGHT
Boy Phones for Help...

"Ben, you do know you can't use a mobile phone while you're in flight, don't you?" asked the lady at the counter as she checked in my bags. She must have read my name on my ticket and recognized it from the newspaper reports. She smiled at Micha, who was pushing Martin in the wheelchair.

I grinned. One of the reporters had already made that joke when we arrived at the airport.

Micha and I were famous. We had been on the front page of newspapers all over New Zealand. Mom and Dad had called and said there had even been a story about us on the evening news back home in America!

Micha had read all the stories to Martin while he was recovering in the hospital. "Boy phones for help while volcano erupts" was just one of the many headlines.

We'd visited Martin a couple of times. The doctors had said we shouldn't fly home right away, so we'd stayed in Auckland for a couple of days.

The first time we visited him in the hospital, he said he wanted to give us his phone to thank us for saving his life.

Boy Phones for Help...

Everyone had laughed when Mrs. Lee pointed out that Martin's phone wouldn't work in the United States.

Mr. Lee added, "You keep it, Martin. That way, any time there's a really good snowfall, you can give us a call!"

I looked over at Micha. She was using a big pen to sign Martin's cast. She was writing something clever like, "Don't ever try skiing in lava!"

Micha was handing the pen to me when Martin's mobile phone rang. Martin answered.

"It's for you, Ben," he said with a big grin on his face.

I looked around at everybody in surprise. Who on Earth would be calling me on Martin's phone?

"Ben Cameron speaking."

"Hi there, Ben," came the friendly voice of Jane Porter, Martin's friend.

"Martin wanted me to make sure you knew how to use a phone. You know, in case you get into any more trouble on your way home!"

"Ha, ha, you guys. That's really funny," I said. Then I moved the phone away from my ear and pressed END.